PRIVATE EYE

BOOK OF COVERS

Published in Great Britain 1978 by
Private Eye Productions Limited
34 Greek Street, London W1.
In association with André Deutsch Limited.
105 Great Russell Street, London WC1.
© Pressdram Limited 1978.
ISBN 233 97044 4

Printed in Great Britain by A. Wheaton & Co., Ltd., Exeter

The First Bubble Cover.

PRIVATE EYE

incorporating THE FLESH'S WEEKLY

VOL I No 4   Wednesday 7th February 1962   Price 6d.

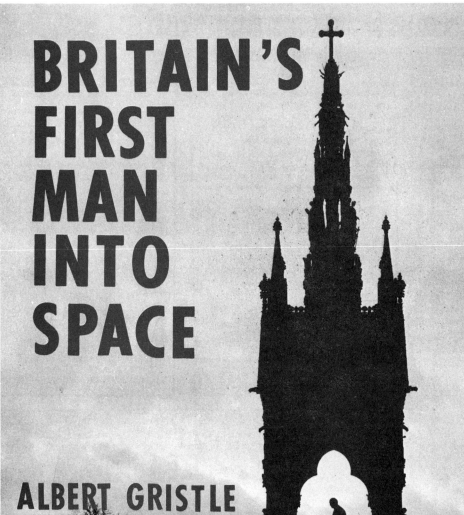

Britain and U.S. continue with
nuclear tests.

PRIVATE EYE

A FORTNIGHTLY LAMPOON

Vol. 1 No. 9   Thursday 19th. April 1962   Price 1/-

TESTING THE WORLD AWAY

Early attack on George Brown.

PRIVATE EYE

A FORTNIGHTLY LAMPOON

Vol. 1 No. 10 | Friday 4th. May 1962 | Price 1/-

The poet Milligan speaks — page 9

Official opening of Coventry cathedral.

PRIVATE EYE

No. 12
Friday
1 June 62

Price 1/-

Selwyn Lloyd, Chancellor of the Exchequer, dismissed in Macmillan purge.

PRIVATE EYE

No. 16
Friday
27 July 62

Price 1/-

De Gaulle vetoes Britain's bid to join the Common Market.

No. 29
Friday
25 January 63

PRIVATE EYE

Price 1/-

Minister of Defence John Profumo
talks to Geoffrey Rippon.

PRIVATE EYE

No. 34
Friday
5 April 63

Price 1/-

Mandy Rice-Davis, star of the
Profumo affair.

PRIVATE EYE

No. 42
Friday
26 July 63

Price 1/-

Do you mind?
If it wasn't for me -
you couldn't have cared
less about Rachman

Publication of the Denning Report on the Profumo affair.

PRIVATE EYE

No 46
Friday
20 Sept. 63

Price 1/-

Gerald Scarfe.

DENNING IS SERVED

Macmillan resigns. 'Old colleague' is R. A. Butler.

Right wing Senator Goldwater
was Republican Candidate in
Presidential Elections.

PRIVATE EYE

No 67
Friday
10 July 64

1/-

WORLD PEACE | GOLDWATER SPEAKS

The Queen reads speech for
Wilson's first Labour government.

PRIVATE EYE

No 75
Friday
30 October 64

1/6

QUEEN OPENS PARLIAMENT

HOW MANY POOVES ARE THERE IN WILSON'S GOVERNMENT?

see page 3.

Wilson publicity stresses humble home life.

PRIVATE EYE

N.S.M.A.P.M.A.F.C.K.U.P.
(SEE P. 13)

No 77
Friday
27 November 64

1/6

HAROLD DRIES UP AT LAST

I wish you'd do this when there AREN'T any photographers around

MRS. WILSON'S DIARY

SEE PAGE 14

Wilson gives uncritical support
to U.S. Vietnamese policy.

PRIVATE EYE

No. 88
Friday
30 April 65

Private Eye Jamboree, St. Pancras Town Hall, May 4th – see page 11.

1/6

VIETNAM

WILSON

RIGHT

BEHIND

JOHNSON

**First Royal visit to Germany
since the war.**

Edward Heath goes on holiday.

PRIVATE EYE

No. 99
Friday
1 Oct. 65

1/6

Wilson develops close ties with Royalty.

PRIVATE EYE

No. 102
Friday
12 Nov. 65

1/6

We can't go on meeting like this

THE QUEEN AND MR WILSON **THE TRUTH**

SEE PAGE 14

First visit by Archbishop of Canterbury
to the Vatican since the Reformation.

PRIVATE EYE

No. 112
Friday,
1 April '66.

1/6

Early photograph of the moon's surface.

PRIVATE EYE

No. 117
Friday,
10 June 66

1/6

The Pound under pressure yet again.

PRIVATE EYE

No. 120
Friday
22 July 66

1/6

YOURS FOR 5/-

(in three months time)

Disillusionment with Labour
Government following Wilson's
'July measures'.

PRIVATE EYE

No. 121
Friday
5 Aug 66

1/6

Assassination of S. African premier Dr Verwoerd.

PRIVATE EYE

No. 124
Friday
17 Sept. 66

1/6

VERWOERD

A NATION
MOURNS

Lord Thomson buys *The Times*.

PRIVATE EYE

No. 126
Friday
14 Oct. 66.

1/6

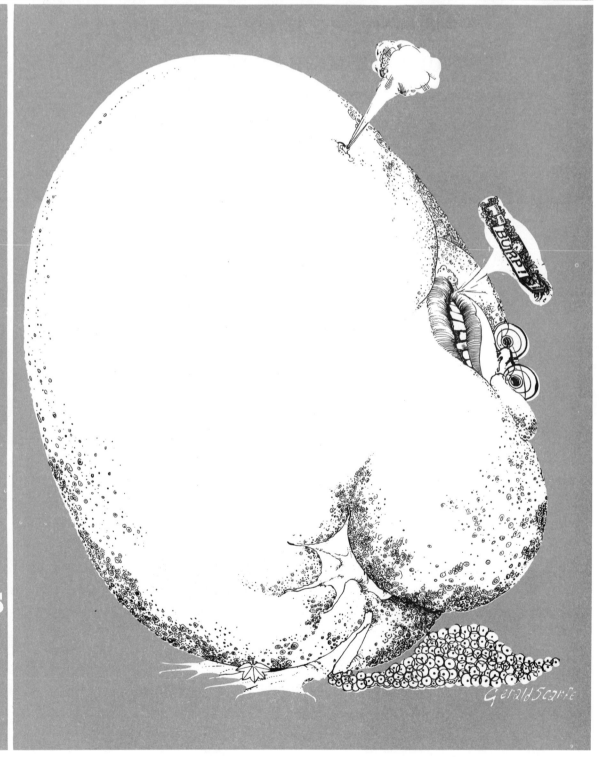

THOMSON
SWALLOWS
THE
TIMES
Amazing
picture

Wilson and Brown investigate
the Common Market.

PRIVATE EYE

No. 134
Friday
3 Feb. 67

1/6

Le seul Journal satirique du Monde

Wilson calls for a 'Great Debate' on the Common Market.

PRIVATE EYE

No. 141.
Friday
12 May 67

1/6

COMMON MARKET

THE GREAT
DEBATE BEGINS

Coloured cricketer Basil D'Oliveira (right) refused admission to S. Africa.

PRIVATE EYE

No. 176
Friday
13 Sept. '68

1/6

Beatle John Lennon on drugs charge.

PRIVATE EYE

No. 179
Friday
25 Oct. '68

1/6

BEATLE HELD

SENSATION

★

SPECIAL REVOLTING ISSUE

All human filth is here

(including Robert Maxwell)

Jackie Kennedy marries
Aristotle Onassis.

PRIVATE EYE

No. 180
Friday
8 Nov. '68

1/6

Richard Nixon becomes U.S. President.
Spiro Agnew is Vice-President.

PRIVATE EYE

No. 182
Friday
6 Dec. '68

1/6

and I tell you some of them have got them this long!

POWELL NEW OUTBURST

Private Eye Editor (left) receives award.

PRIVATE EYE

No. 185
Friday
17 Jan. '69

1/6

WINNER OF *GRANADA TV* 'IRRITANT OF THE YEAR' AWARD

Ian Paisley (centre) emerges as leader of hard line Ulster protestants.

PRIVATE EYE

No. 189
Friday
14 March
'69   2/-

Callaghan makes abortive anti-Wilson coup.

PRIVATE EYE

No. 191
Friday
11 April 69

2/-

Euthanasia controversy.

PRIVATE EYE

No. 193
Friday
9 May 69

2/-

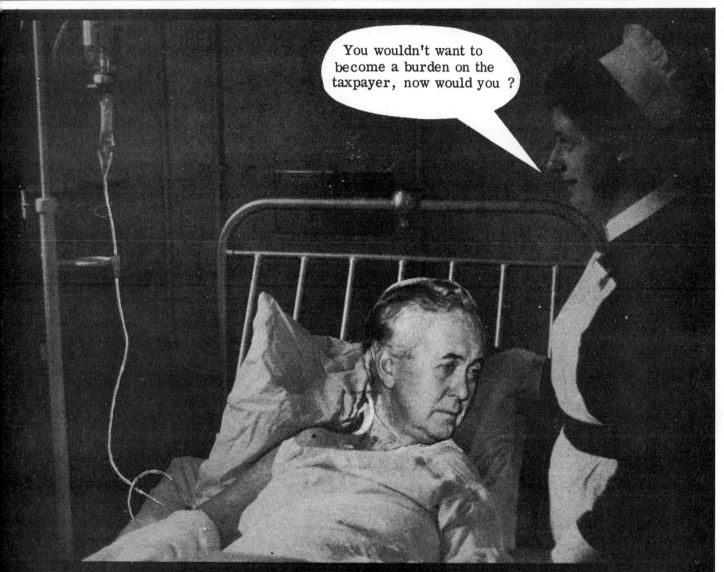

SHOULD THIS MAN BE KEPT ALIVE?

Chauvinist crudity.

PRIVATE EYE

No. 194
Friday
23 May '69

The Queen is acclaimed for her performance in a television documentary.

PRIVATE EYE

No. 197
Friday
4 July 69

2/-

QUEEN TOPS TV POPS

Ulster's Bernadette Devlin visits America.

PRIVATE EYE

No. 202
Friday
12 Sept. 69

2/-

General Election 1970, won by Heath.

PRIVATE EYE

No. 220
Friday
22 May '70

2/-

I never thought he could pull it off three times running

You've never had it so good

and I've never had it!

THEY'RE OFF!

(OR NOT - as this issue went to press before any announcement was made)

Rumours of disharmony at
Kensington Palace.

PRIVATE EYE

No. 226
Friday
14 Aug. '70.

2/-

TONY & MARGARET —The Truth

Mick Jagger weds Bianca in France.

PRIVATE EYE

No. 246
Friday
21 May '71

10p

THAT WEDDING

SOUVENIR ISSUE

Visit to Britain of Japanese Emperor.

PRIVATE EYE

Ah so's to you, too matey!

No. 256
Friday
8 Oct. '71

10p

Thalidomide parents sue Distillers Co.

PRIVATE EYE

No. 285
Friday
17 Nov.'72

10p

THALIDOMIDE CASE

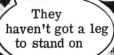

They haven't got a leg to stand on

SIR ALEX McDONALD
Chairman Distillers

Chairman's Statement

Cyril Smith (left) elected for Rochdale.

PRIVATE EYE

No. 287
Friday
15 Dec. '72

10p

LIBERAL REVIVAL

The Watergate Scandal.

PRIVATE EYE

No. 297
Friday
4 May '73

12p

Vice-President Spiro Agnew resigns.

PRIVATE EYE

No. 309
Friday
19 Oct. '73

12p

Agnew and Nixon

The Last Fare~well

Goodbye Sir

AAARGH!

Marcia Williams given life peerage.

PRIVATE EYE

No. 325
Friday
31 May '74

12p

IT'S LADY SLAGHEAP!

WILSON'S SHOCKER

I.R.A. funeral procession in Kilburn.

PRIVATE IRA

No. 326
Friday
14 June '74

12p

SPONSORED WALK
HELP THE BLIND

Edward Heath loses election
and comes under fire.

PRIVATE EYE

No. 335
Friday
18 Oct. '74

12p

TORIES CONSIDER HEATH'S FUTURE

Arab influence grows.

PRIVATE EYE

No. 340
Friday
10 Jan. '75

12p

BRITAIN SOLD SHOCK

My wives and I . .

New Man at Palace

President Amin makes joke.

PRIVATE EYE

No. 353
Friday
7 June '75

15p

Runaway M.P. John Stonehouse
brought back to Britain.

PRIVATE EYE

No. 355
Friday
25th July '75

15p

STONEHOUSE FLIES IN

Which way to the beach ?

North Sea Oil begins to flow.

PRIVATE EYE

No. 363
Friday
14 Nov. '75

15p

Now British Oil.

Inaugural flight of Concorde.

PRIVATE EYE

No. 368
Friday
23 Jan. '76

15p

UP AND AWAY !

Will the passenger
please fasten his
safety belt

It's the Bahrain
Drain !

Reports of Princess Margaret's
romance with playboy
Roddy Llewellyn.

PRIVATE EYE

No. 371
Friday
5 March '76

15p

QUEEN IN FLEET ST.

EXCLUSIVE PICTURE

Harold Wilson resigns.

PRIVATE EYE

No. 373
Friday
2 April '76

15p

END OF AN ERA

Alright, Jim, you can take over now

Roy Jenkins leaves Labour Government
for Common Market Commission,
following election of Callaghan.

PRIVATE EYE

No. 374
Friday
16 April '76

15p

Jeremy Thorpe, liberal leader, resigns.

PRIVATE EYE

No. 376
Friday
May '76

15p

THORPE RESIGNS SHOCK

Any chance of a life peerage, Harold ?

I doubt it. You're not her type

President Ford makes fatal gaffe.

PRIVATE EYE

No. 396
Friday
18 Feb. '77

20p

Wilson and Maudling both beneficiaries of crooked property man Sir Eric Miller who committed suicide.

PRIVATE EYE

No. 412
Friday
30 Sept. '77

20p

President Sadat makes historic trip to Israel.

PRIVATE EYE

No.416
Friday
25 Nov.'77

25p

WIND OF CHANGE IN MIDDLE EAST